Riverbank Stories

- O N E - .

The Tale of Jeremy Vole

Riverbank Stories

- O N E -

The Tale of
Jeremy Vole

Stephen Lawhead

A LION BOOK

Oxford · Batavia · Sydney

Copyright © 1990 Stephen Lawhead

Published by
Lion Publishing Corporation
1705 Hubbard Avenue, Batavia, Illinois 60510, USA
ISBN 0 7459 1653 8
Lion Publishing plc
Sandy Lane West, Oxford, England
ISBN 0 7459 1653 8
Albatross Books Pty Ltd
PO Box 320, Sutherland, NSW 2232, Australia
ISBN 0 7324 0200 X

First edition 1990

Reprinted 1991

Library of Congress Cataloging in Publication Data

Lawhead, Stephen
 The tale of Jeremy Vole / Stephen. Lawhead.
 p.   cm. — (Riverbank stories)
 ISBN 0-7459-1653-8
 [1. Animals—Fiction.]   I. Title   II. Series
PZ7.L41847Tal   1990
[Fic]—dc20

British Library Cataloguing in Publication Data

Lawhead, Stephen, 1950–
 The tale of Jeremy Vole.
 I. Title   II. Series
 813'.54 [J]

 ISBN 0-7459-1653-8

Printed in United States of America

CONTENTS

1

A Message from the Blue

Jeremy Vole lived in a hole. He lived in a hole in the bank of a canal. Nothing exciting ever happened to him, and that's the way he liked it. Excitement made him nervous. It made him itch. He preferred life to just glide along calmly and smoothly without a ripple.

He did not like trouble. He did not like surprises. He did not like much of anything except his own warm, dry hole in the riverbank, and staying there. Indeed, a more stay-at-homebody could not be found anywhere. He loved his little house and everything in it. A more perfect home he could not imagine. With a warm snug den, a roomy pantry chock full of good things to eat, a big snug bed of finest hand-picked thistledown – it was the place he loved best in all the world. Jeremy Vole was one house-proud little vole.

The only time he poked his nose out of doors was when he went for his morning swim – which was the only other thing that he liked.

Early one spring morning Jeremy awoke, rolled out of his fine bed, and slipped quietly into the canal outside his front door. The water was cool and calm – best of all he had it all to himself. No other Riverbank creature was stirring on this glistening morning.

He swam for a while on his stomach, which he always did while paddling upstream. Then he turned around and swam on his back, which he always did while drifting downstream – careful not to stray too far from home lest he get swept into the swifter current where the canal joined the wider River at the Gas Bridge a few hundred paces farther along.

Well, here was Jeremy puttering along, minding his own business when WHUMP! BUMP! he swam smack into two long poles sticking out of the water where no poles ought to be.

"Hello!" he said. "What have we here?"

As he spoke, his beady little eyes travelled up the long length of the poles to see the body of a bird perched at the very top: an enormous, keen-eyed, long-necked, sharp-beaked, stilt-legged bird. A heron. And no ordinary one, at that.

9

Jeremy was not exactly sure whether herons ate voles or not. He dimly remembered a twice-great uncle (or was it a fourth cousin once removed?) who had a disagreement with a heron (or was it an owl?) and wound up as elevenses (or was it tea?) – Jeremy didn't know. But however it was, it had ended badly.

Quick as a blink, Jeremy dived under the water. He stayed down as long as he could, but after a little while he had to come up for a breath of air. The heron was still there.

"You there! Vole!" called the top-lofty bird in a deep voice. "Come here, I wish to speak to you."

"I won't! You mean to eat me!" Jeremy piped.

"Of course I'm not going to eat you. I want to talk to you. Come closer."

Jeremy shook his head and prepared to dive again.

The heron fixed a stern and commanding eye upon little Jeremy. "If I had wanted to eat you, I would have done so the moment I saw you. Now, stop this silliness and come here. I have a message for you."

"For me? You have a message for me?"

"Yes, you. I have a job for you."

"A job? For me?"

"Must I say everything twice?" said the big bird. "Come closer."

"Yes?" said Jeremy, feeling that he was quite close enough already.

"Closer," said the heron. "I am growing hoarse for shouting."

Cautiously, Jeremy paddled to a nearby branch which drooped close to the water. He did not like the heron's sharp eye, or sharper beak. But there was something unusual about this heron that roused his curiosity. So he plucked up his courage and scampered up onto the branch. "You said something about a job, I believe," he said.

"Have you a name, Vole?"

"Jeremy," replied our little soggy friend.

"Capital! Now then, listen carefully, Jeremy. What I am going to say, I will say but once. Do you understand?"

"Not really," admitted Jeremy. "But do continue and I will try to catch up as you go."

"You do that," the bird said. "Ready?"

Jeremy squinted up his eyes and took the tip of his tail in his front feet – all the better to hear. "Ready."

"In a little while," intoned the bird solemnly, "there is coming a great disaster to this river – "

"Oh, my!" Jeremy dropped his tail so he could

scratch his ear which had developed a sudden itch.

The heron ruffled his feathers and continued, " – a disaster in the form of a terrible flood. It will be the worst flood seen on this river in a hundred years. Do you understand?"

"The worst flood in a hundred years," repeated the vole. "Yes, I think I have it."

"Good," replied the heron gravely. "Now this is the most important part: you must warn the other creatures of Riverbank. It is up to you, Jeremy Vole, to save them."

Jeremy almost fell off his branch. "Me?" he gasped. "How?"

"However you wish," the heron answered. "This is the job I have chosen for you. It will not be easy, but these things rarely are."

"Easy? Why . . . why – " sputtered Jeremy, completely forgetting himself, "it's impossible!"

"Very likely," admitted the bird, stretching his long, slender wings. "But there you are."

"Why me?"

"Because you are here," the heron told him. "And, to tell you the truth, I can think of no better reason than that."

"But – but . . ."

"Besides, I like you."

13

"But!" said the vole yet again, for emphasis.

"Do not fret, Jeremy. Be of good cheer. My most sincere best wishes go with you."

"But who are you?" asked the vole.

"Don't you know me yet?" The mysterious bird began flapping his wings with such force that the vole was nearly blown off his branch. "I am the Great Blue Heron." Then, lifting his long stilt legs, the huge bird took several running steps across the water and lifted himself into the air.

Jeremy sat on his branch, scratching his itchy hide as the heron disappeared into the morning mist. And he thought he heard the voice of the Great Blue drifting back to him, saying, "Hur-r-r-y . . . No-o time to lo-o-o-o-se . . ."

2

Losing No Time

Jeremy shook his furry little head and hurried back to his hole. Ah, safe at home! No disturbing birds could bother him here. His cosy den did not admit sharp-beaked strangers bearing alarming news of floods. In his house Jeremy was king; he did as he pleased. And he certainly did not please to think about wild-eyed errands.

"What I need is breakfast," he said to himself and went to his pantry to find a nice plump horse-radish. Nothing like a savoury root to make a fellow forget his troubles. But, as he tucked into his meal, he could not help thinking about what he had seen and heard.

And what he thought was this:

How can I be sure it really was the Great Blue Heron? He had never seen a Blue Heron before. So how did he know he had seen one now?

Maybe it was a really a Grey Heron. Of course! That's what it was, a silly old Grey.

But it *wasn't* grey. It was blue. And big. And then there was the part about the terrible flood. He didn't know what to make of that.

It was, Jeremy decided, a most peculiar business. Most peculiar. Well, there was only one thing to do: take a nap. After that, he would see how things stood.

Creeping over to his fine soft bed of thistle fluff, he curled up in a bristly ball and wrapped his tail around his toes. Unfortunately, every time he closed his eyes he saw floods. And not small floods, either: large, terrible floods – tidal waves of angry water, all black and frothy, and roaring through Riverbank in a fury.

And he heard again the Great Blue's warning: *It is up to you to save them*, and *Hurry! No time to lose!*

It occurred to Jeremy that the Blue had been mistaken. Surely, this was a job for someone in authority. Of course, why hadn't he thought of it before? He would go and see Bodger Badger, Lord Mayor of Riverbank. After all, wasn't taking care of such problems exactly the sort of thing the Mayor was supposed to do?

But seeing the Mayor would mean leaving his house. Jeremy hated going out at this time of day.

Actually, he hated going out any time of day. And Mayor Badger lived on the other side of Water Meadow, and getting there would mean leaving the canal and taking to River. Jeremy absolutely loathed leaving the canal. River was no place for a vole; it was too busy, and too crowded.

Once he had been swept into River by mistake and carried downstream to Folly Bridge. He had to walk all that long way back home and had been chased by a bad yellow cat named Boris. That had been altogether too much excitement. He itched for a week.

Still, it couldn't be helped. To see the Mayor he'd have to chance River. Reluctantly, Jeremy peeped out of his den. No one was about. Good. He took a deep breath, slithered down the bank, and chugged off to find Bodger Badger.

Jeremy soon reached the place where the canal and River met. He plucked up his courage and steamed off. It was early yet; river traffic was still a notch or two below fever pitch. So Jeremy arrived at Mayor Badger's den at the edge of Water Meadow with his wits about him and his furry little skin intact.

Jeremy rapped politely at the Badger's rock-lined door and began pressing the water from his fur while he waited. Soon he heard someone

stirring and, a moment later, out poked the Lord Mayor's nose.

"Oh, hello Vole," the Mayor said. "Jeremy – isn't it?"

"That's right," replied the vole, flattered that the Lord Mayor remembered his name.

"Never forget a face, that's me for you." Bodger Badger waddled out of his den and began grooming his handsome black-and-white striped fur. "What seems to be the trouble? Rates gone up? Council got you by the throat?"

"Not exactly, Lord Mayor," began Jeremy, "it's just that – "

"Now, before you begin, I think I should warn you that I've a very busy schedule just at the moment. Quite a lot on my plate, don't you know. I'll thank you to make it brief – it'll save us both a world of time. There's a good chap."

"Well, I seem to have – "

"Of course you have!" cried the Mayor. "Haven't we all? It's nothing to be ashamed of. Why, I've even been known – not as a general habit, you understand, but from time to time, sort of thing – to have a go myself. Good for you, Vole! That's what I say! Good for you!"

The badger stuck his nose in the air and sniffed. "Well, well, what a day! So much to do, so little time! Thank you, Vole, I can't say how much I've appreciated this little chat. But then, that's what I'm here for. I always have time for my friends, don't you know. Now then, I really must be going! Tara!"

The Lord Mayor retreated into his den, leaving his visitor blinking in the sun. Jeremy was still sitting there, trying to work up his nerve to go back into River, when Wrigglesworth Rabbit came bounding up.

"Hi-Ho! Top o' the morning to you, J.V. Beautiful day, what?"

"Hello, Riggs. Yes, I suppose it is."

"What's up, old son? Been to see the Mayor?"

"Yes and no," answered Jeremy. "I saw him, but I don't think he saw me."

"I know what you mean, old bean. Politicians! Tch! I wouldn't give you a tin tuppence for the lot."

"It's just that I've got this problem. I don't know what to do about it."

The rabbit regarded him with a sympathetic brown eye. "In a jam, sport? You want to get expert advice."

"Expert advice?"

"Righty ho! Go and see an expert; hire a consultant. It's the done thing. Everything but everything is run by experts. Those chaps'll see you right."

"Well, I don't know – " began the vole.

"Believe me, you're miles ahead with a bit of expert advice under your bonnet." The rabbit stretched his long hind legs. "I'm off for a jog, care to join me?"

"Sorry, I can't jog."

"Pity – do you good. Anyway, nice to see you, Jeremy. Come by the club some time. We'll have lunch. Cheerio!" And the rabbit raced away.

"Maybe Riggs is right," thought Jeremy. "Maybe an expert is what I need."

With that thought fixed firmly in his head, the vole slipped back into the water and stroked off to find himself an expert.

Expert Advice

Jeremy took his search for an expert to the door of his friend, Alfred Hedgehog, who lived under the roots of a blackthorn bush near the tow path on the other side of River. Alfred was the brainiest thing going. Always nose down in a bit of book or shred of newspaper, the prickly hedgehog was as much of an expert as Riverbank could boast.

As luck would have it, Alfred was just returning from his nightly ramble as Jeremy trotted up. "Oh, hullo there, Jeremy. You are looking chipper this morning. Care for a cricket?"

"No thank you, Alfred. But do go right ahead. It's just that I need a bit of advice." And Jeremy began explaining about the heron and the flood and the rabbit's suggestion to take the problem to an expert. "So that's why I've come to *you*, Alfred," he said as he finished.

The hedgehog munched thoughtfully for a

moment, considering the problem from several perspectives, numerous positions, and not a few points of view. "Yes, well . . ." the hedgehog said. And, "Well now, yes indeed . . ." and "Hmmm, I wonder . . ."

Jeremy knew these were thinking sounds and did not interrupt. He sat quietly stroking his fur with his front feet to make it smooth and shimmery.

"The main thing, it seems to me," announced Alfred Hedgehog suddenly, "is that this information comes to you in a highly eccentric manner and from an exceedingly unreliable source. That makes it spurious."

"Eccentric? Unreliable? Spurious? Whatever do you mean?" asked Jeremy, for Alfred always used big confusing words where small simple ones would do.

"The Great Blue Heron – that is what I mean."

"Yes? What about him?"

"He is what is known as an impeachable source."

"A what?"

"A phoney. A fraud. A figment of your imagination. Or words to that effect. Have you ever heard of a Great Blue Heron in these parts? Of course not – they don't exist."

"Oh."

"You have to look at it scientifically, dear fellow," explained Alfred, and reached for an earthworm. "By the way, are you sure I can't offer you anything? An important source of protein, worms."

"No, thank you," replied Jeremy, looking doubtfully at the worm. "I couldn't. But do carry on."

"Very well," said Alfred, popping the worm into his mouth. "Now then, where was I?"

"Looking at it scientifically?"

"Ah, yes. Science is everything, Jeremy. Quite literally everything. The world will realize that one day. Take this flood of yours – "

"It isn't *my* flood," protested Jeremy.

"But how do you know? Did a weatherman tell you? Or any kind of scientist at all? Someone from the Thames Water Authority? The lock-keeper, perhaps? Or an official from the Milk Board?"

Jeremy shook his head. "Of course not. The Great Blue Heron told me."

"Twaddle! You don't mean to tell me you actually believe in this Great Blue Heron poppycock?"

"Well, I – "

"I'm surprised at you, Jeremy. Really, you might at least have checked the tide tables. Instead, you took the word of a – a rather confused bird."

"He wasn't confused. He was blue."

"Same thing, dear fellow. Facts! Facts are what count in a case like this. Incontrovertible evidence!"

"In-con-tra-WHAT-ible?"

"Solid."

"Oh," sighed Jeremy unhappily. "Well, thank you for your help, Alfred. I won't keep you from your sleep."

"Always a pleasure, Jeremy. Any time, any time." Alfred Hedgehog shuffled into his burrow. "Ah, science . . ."

Now what? wondered Jeremy. His expert made it all sound very simple. There was no flood, because there was no proof, because the heron was a peach . . . or words to that effect.

Alfred was probably right. What proof could he offer for this flood business? None – except the word of a great peculiar heron.

What good was that? Not much at all, reflected Jeremy. And he was of a mind to go right back to his snug home and forget the whole confusing business when he slid into the water and bumped nose-first into Polly Frog.

26

Of Frogs and
Flying Saucers

"Bless me, it's Jeremy!" chirped Polly, winking her big yellow eyes. "Fancy bumping into you."

"Oh, hello, Polly," muttered Jeremy. "Nice day, isn't it?"

"Couldn't tell to look at you. Why so down in the mouth, love?"

Jeremy took a deep breath and told the frog all about the Great Blue Heron and the flood and the expert advice. When he finished, she nodded sympathetically. "Oh, I know what you mean. My old grandmum saw a flying saucer once – blue flashing lights and a shrieky noise something awful – nearly scared her spots off."

"I don't think this is the same thing at all," began Jeremy. But before he could explain, Polly jumped in again.

"And then there was the time my Ferd mistook

a bit of swamp gas for the ghost of his Uncle Thaddeus."

"This was different," insisted Jeremy. "There really *was* a Great Blue Heron."

"That's what Grandmum said, too. To her dying day she insisted the Blue Thingies would come back and take her to Florida."

"That's very interesting, Polly . . ." the vole said slowly, backing away. He said good-day and continued on his way.

But Alfred and Polly had started Jeremy thinking. Had he simply imagined the heron? Was it only a bit of mist, a wisp of fog and river murk, a bluish haze?

If so, it was a mist with muscle! A wisp with a will! Imagined or not, the bluish haze had spoken to him. It had called him by name. And it had given him a job to do, a mission.

But how to do it? That was the tricky bit.

What I need is a plan, Jeremy thought. What I need is a scheme. What I need is a *snack*, he decided at last, and struck off towards home.

Along the way, however, he was passed by a fleet of ducks, racing upstream along the canal. He recognized one of them and called out. "Malcolm! Oh, Malcolm!"

A big mallard peeled away from the fleet and came skidding over the water. "Ho, Jeremy! Can't stop now – there's a hamper overturned at Osney Lock!"

"A picnic hamper?"

"First of the year! And a big one, too. I hear there might be a jam tart! Maybe some short-bread!"

"Oh! Well, I won't keep you . . . It's just – "

"Right! I'm off."

Jeremy watched the duck steaming away and it came to him that where there was a picnic basket there was sure to be a crowd. What better place to deliver his message? Of course! He could go and do his bit, once and for all.

That's it! Speak to the crowd, tell everybody about the flood, and let that be the end of it. Then he could go home and never come out again if he didn't feel like it. Certainly, this was the answer to his problem.

"Malcolm! Hey, Malcolm, wait for me!" The vole put his head down and splashed after the big mallard.

Jeremy swam downstream a while, and soon arrived at the place where the canal met River. He looked at the wide water, swallowed hard, and plunged ahead. "Oh dear, twice in one day!"

he muttered. "I hope this isn't getting to be a habit!"

Keeping close to the shoreline, he paddled along, ears flat to his head, the tip of his nose high above the water. He swam a long, long time, and at last came to a place where River turned and rounded a bend. He journeyed on, and in a little while saw the Osney Lock footbridge in the distance.

He could see a crowd gathered on the water beneath the bridge. And others – swans whistling in from the sky, ducks skimming across the water, fish zig-zagging through the rippling waves – all of them racing to the overturned hamper. It was a fair-sized picnic basket, too – one of those posh wicker affairs that the city folk sometimes took with them on country outings. Little wonder that half the creatures of Riverbank had come to join the feast.

The vole swam on and soon noticed unopened bags of crisps floating past like little pillows – salt and vinegar, bacon, prawn, and onion. He saw boiled eggs bobbing by, plastic yoghurt tubs, a packet of ginger cream biscuits, and a bottle of Quosh! He ignored these treasures and continued full steam ahead.

Such a feast! Such excitement! So much food

and so many creatures causing such a fuss and flurry. Entirely too much of a fuss and flurry for Jeremy. One look, and his nose began to itch. He began having second thoughts, and then third thoughts. His feet prickled and his tail began to sting.

"Maybe," Jeremy mused, stopping to scratch himself, "this plan could do with one or two small adjustments. No sense in being hasty." The more he thought about it, the more he saw he was right. Yes, a short pause to sort it all out was definitely in order. Of course! Silly not to have thought of it before.

So he pulled up a short way from the picnic hamper to have a look at Where Things Stood. It appeared to Jeremy for all the world as if he'd happened upon a water-borne blizzard, what with ducks and swans and swooping gulls flapping all over the place. Feathers filled the air! And the squawk!

Now his ears began to itch. "This is beastly," he thought, scratching away. "I'm not about to get mixed up with that rowdy lot!" He turned right around and paddled for home.

He hadn't stroked very far, however, when he seemed to hear the Blue Heron's stern voice in his ear saying, *"It will be the worst flood seen on this* river in a hundred years. *You must warn the other creatures of Riverbank. It is up to you, Jeremy Vole, to save them."*

"Why, oh why?" sighed Jeremy. "Why does it have to be me?"

He stopped and peered back over his shoulder. Well, best to get it over with, he thought. That's right, screw courage to the sticking place, grit teeth, and do the deed.

So Jeremy put his head down and dived straight into the heart of the hub-bub. Of all the things he might have done, that was probably the worst.

5

Feeding Frenzy

Jeremy squirmed and wriggled his way to the picnic basket. No mean feat, for there was so much jostling, fighting and shoving he could scarcely move for getting cuffed and buffed about.

"Back! Back!" a ring-necked duck squawked loudly in his ear. "I was here first!"

"Sorry!" replied Jeremy politely.

"Oi! Give over!" shouted someone else. "You're in my way!"

"So sorry!" Jeremy spun around.

"Watch it, bussster!" hissed a swan, flapping his wings and swinging his long neck towards the vole. "Queue jumper!"

"I have as much right to be here as anybody!" Jeremy told him, and nearly lost an ear. He dived out of sight just as the swan's bill snipped the air where his head had been.

"This will never do," thought Jeremy, as he dived into a mass of swarming, darting fish. "They'll never hear me in all this ruckus. How can I make them listen?"

As he dodged among the churning feet of the ducks and swans, an idea came to him. He swam to the edge of the hamper and hung on to it. Gripping the wicker with his wiry little toes, he pulled himself aboard.

Before anyone noticed, he had scampered up the side of the floating picnic basket and perched himself on top of the handle. "Friends!" he shouted. "Listen to me!"

This surprised everybody, and for a moment the feeding frenzy stopped. "Oh!" Jeremy gasped when he saw everyone staring at him. "Oh, I – ah, yes . . . it's just that . . . well, there was this heron, you see . . . and I, that is, he, the heron, I mean – "

"What's he doing up there?" demanded a swan.

"You there!" shouted another. "What are you doing up there?"

"Is this some kind of joke?" shrieked a seagull.

"Please," said Jeremy, "I saw the Great Blue Heron and – "

"Bully for you!" sneered one of the ducks.

"Shove off!" yelled another, moving closer.

"But there's a flood coming!" cried Jeremy desperately. "A terrible flood, and it's – "

"Haw, haw, haw!" shrieked a gull, and just for spite flew down and pecked Jeremy square on the head. "There's a joke for you!" Everyone laughed, the seagull most of all.

"Ow!" squeaked Jeremy. "It's not a joke! It's true! Ow!"

One of the ducks – Jeremy's friend Malcolm – swam to the hamper. "Jeremy?" he whispered. "What on earth are you doing? Get down from there. Come on, before you get yourself hurt."

"I'm trying to get their attention," Jeremy said.

"I think you've done that," said Malcolm. "Maybe it's time to leave."

"When I'm finished," replied the vole.

"You're finished," Malcolm assured him. "Believe me."

"Not until I'm finished talking."

"Well," sighed Malcolm, backing away slowly, "I hope you finish talking soon, because I think they're finished listening."

"Now what's he doing?" shouted someone from the rear.

"He's ruining our feast!" shrieked the gull, swooping dangerously near.

"Please listen, for pity's sake!" cried Jeremy.

"Hear that? He's after the fairy cakes!" bellowed a big drake. "Let's get him!"

All at once, two or three seagulls dived at Jeremy and knocked him into the water. The feeding frenzy started again and Jeremy was shoved rudely aside. He looked on for a moment, then turned and began making his long, slow way back home.

Tea and Sympathy

Jeremy spent the rest of the day, and most of the next, tucked up in bed nursing his wounds. His head hurt where the gull had pecked him; his sides ached where he had been buffeted around. And, thanks to all the excitement, he now itched from the end of his whiskered nose to the pink tippy-tip of his tail – and everywhere else in between. He had fairly scratched himself raw!

The maddening itch was bad enough. Worse was the shame. He had made a fool of himself. All of Riverbank was probably laughing at him right now. He could scratch the itch, but he couldn't stop the laughter. And that was what hurt the most.

"Poor me," he moaned. "Poor, poor me." This sighing and moaning did not help nearly as much as he might have wished. There was surprisingly little comfort in feeling sorry for himself. Less, at any rate, than he'd hoped.

In the end, Jeremy arrived at the conclusion that it was not self-pity that he wanted, it was sympathy. The best place for sympathy, he decided, was over tea. And the best place for a cup of hot tea was with his good friend Herkimer.

"Ol' Herky makes a top-rate cuppa," Jeremy said to himself, feeling a touch better already. "I'll just pop over to see him."

Herkimer Housebound lived in a mud cave up the canal, near the Oxpens Bridge. It was a good place, peaceful and quiet, with reeds and rushes and river grass growing along the water's edge. It was one of Riverbank's more desirable residences. A pair of swans lived nearby, making their nest in the long grass. Herkimer had a nice flat rock at the edge of the canal where he liked to sun himself. This is where Jeremy found him, fast asleep.

"Hello! Hello there, Herky!"

The turtle slowly raised his wrinkled eyelids. "Oh, ahhh, yes," he said. "Who is it?"

"It's me, Jeremy," the vole said, puttering up to the rock. "Your friend from down the way."

"Bless me, so it is! Long time no see, Jeremy Boy," said the turtle.

Herkimer was very rare, and very ancient. Rare, because he was the only turtle anyone had ever known. Ancient, because he was by far the oldest creature in Riverbank – except for the Old Trout, who was so old that nobody now alive knew how old he really was. And if the Old Trout remembered, he wasn't telling. Anyway, Herkimer was ancient enough to call everybody 'boy' or 'girl' or 'kiddy', because to him they were mere youngsters no matter how grown-up they were.

"Greetings, Herky. Am I disturbing you?"

"Bless me, no! Not in the least. I was merely composing an, er – essay. Yes, an essay on the . . . ah, Fundamental Differences Between . . . ah, One Thing and . . . ah, Another Thing."

"That sounds important. I shouldn't like to bother you. Perhaps I ought to come back."

"Not at all. No bother at all. There! You see? I've completely forgotten all about it. So it couldn't have been important. Do sit down."

"Very kind of you," replied Jeremy thoughtfully. "Still, I don't want to keep you from your tea or anything."

"Never!" said the turtle, then wondered, "But is it tea-time already? Bless me, how time flies! Like a rocket!" He raised his wrinkled old head and looked around. "I only closed my eyes for a moment . . . Ahh, me . . . Well, well."

"That's all right then," Jeremy continued, after a small pause. "I know how unexpected guests can sometimes cause such a fuss – especially when it's time for tea."

"Tea? . . . dear me, yes," said the turtle. "Do let's have some tea. Will you join me? But I suppose you're in a hurry. Too bad. Everyone rushes around so these days. Well, perhaps some other time then, eh? Some other time, yes . . . no doubt it's just as well." The turtle laid his head down again and closed one eye.

"As it happens," offered Jeremy hopefully, "I've nothing particularly pressing at the moment. I believe I might stay, if you don't mind. A little tea sounds just the thing."

"Tea!" The turtle snapped. "Bless me! I was just about to have some tea. Would you care to join me, friend Vole?"

"Why, I'd be delighted," replied Jeremy politely.

"Then come along, come along." The turtle slowly eased himself off the rock and into the water. He swam to the bank, pulled himself up the muddy slope, and slipped into his cave. Jeremy followed him in and sat down. While Herkimer busied himself in the pantry, Jeremy

pressed the water from his fur and remarked what a fine den the turtle enjoyed and how it must be a nice snug place to hibernate in winter.

Herkimer hummed busily to himself and returned in a little while with three walnut shells and a mass of dried tangleweed which he placed before his guest. "Here we are. Tea for me and thee. Drink up!"

Jeremy picked up his nutshell and sipped a bit. "Mmmm!"

"It may be a trifle strong," Herkimer warned him. "It's nettle tea. Have a little parsley milk – I find that tames it down nicely."

The turtle tipped some milk into Jeremy's shell, and Jeremy sipped again. "Ahh!" he sighed. "That's better."

Herkimer drank down his tea and regarded Jeremy with a calm, unblinking stare. "Now then," he said slowly, "tell old Herky what's on your mind. More than tea and tangleweed, I expect."

Jeremy blushed and smiled blandly. "Why should anything be the matter?"

"Dear boy, I'll tell you why. Nobody comes to see Herkimer Housebound unless they've a difficulty. You are in a pickle, Jeremy Vole. Old Herkimer can smell a pickle at a thousand paces."

"Now that you mention it," Jeremy confessed, "there is one small thing. I seem to have behaved rather rashly and now all of Riverbank is laughing at me."

"Laughing at you? All of Riverbank? You exaggerate, Jeremy boy. Am I laughing?" The wise old turtle settled down and pulled his feet into his shell. "I think there's more that you're not telling me. Now then, why not tell Herky the trouble? There's a good chap."

The vole took a last sip of his tea and began. "Well, there was a picnic hamper overturned at Osney Lock and I knew it would draw a crowd so I went to warn them about the flood, but they thought I wanted to steal the fairy cakes so they all got angry and started to peck at me and . . ." The words came out in such a rush and tumble that it was a moment before he could stop himself. "I'm not explaining very well, am I?"

"Ahh, no," Herkimer agreed. "Might I suggest you begin at the beginning. And do take your time." He poured more tea into the walnut shells, and smiled. "No need to hurry, we've all the time in the world."

So Jeremy took a deep breath and said very slowly, "I've seen a heron."

"Good for you, Jeremy Boy! A rare treat, I'd say.

A heron – think of it. I saw a wolf once. Magnificent beast. The woods used to be full of them, you know. Haven't been any around here in years. Pity."

"It wasn't any old heron," Jeremy said. "It was the Great Blue Heron."

The turtle opened his eyes wide in surprise. "Was it, by Jove? Bless me! That's something else again. Yes, I say. Something else entirely. Tell me more."

Jeremy did. He told the turtle all: about the heron's message, about the warning, about the flood, about the task he'd been given of warning all the creatures of Riverbank. Herkimer listened, nodding his wrinkled head and blinking slowly.

"So there it is," the vole said, when he finished. "I've told you everything."

"Not quite everything," said the turtle. "You haven't said what you intend to do."

"But that's the point! I don't *know* what to do! That's why I came here. I thought you might help me."

"Very kind of you to think of me," replied Herkimer. "But I cannot help you any more than I already have."

"But you haven't helped me at all!" blurted Jeremy, without thinking.

"I gave you tea and I listened to you," pointed out the turtle patiently. "And I believe you, too. That is all I can do, I think." He thought for a moment. "Yes, that's about it."

"Couldn't you at least tell me what I ought to do?" insisted Jeremy.

"Very risky business that – telling folks what they ought to do. Makes them crabby. No, Jeremy, I like you too much to make you cross with me."

"Mightn't you like me a little less and just give me a hint?"

"Jeremy, Jeremy," sighed the turtle, "the Great Blue Heron chose you, not me."

"But I don't understand. Why choose me at all? There are others so much better at this sort of thing than I am."

"The heron chooses whom he will, for reasons of his own," answered the wise old turtle. "Besides, I think you already know what to do – the Great Blue has told you: warn all of Riverbank about the flood."

Jeremy thanked Herkimer for the tea and said goodbye. He crawled from the turtle's cave and poked his head outside. It was dark and the wind had come up, blowing the branches of the trees so that they clicked against one another. The air was heavy and wet.

The vole slipped silently into the water and began paddling for home. Just as he reached his own snug hole in the bank he heard the far-off grumble of thunder.

7

Snake Logic

Some time during the night the rain began. Jeremy slept, snug in his thistledown, and did not stir until morning, when he woke to the gentle patter of raindrops splashing all around, soaking into the earth, running down in small trickles into the canal . . . *Flood!*

Jeremy leaped out of bed, flew out of his den, slid down the muddy bank and fell PLOP! into the water. He bobbed up in the middle of a bunch of ducks.

"Look out, it's the crazy vole!" shouted the leader. "Hey, Jeremy, don't let the big bad flood get you!" And they all laughed.

As the ducks moved off, one of the group swam near. It was Malcolm. "Just a bit of fun, Jeremy. Don't take on so."

"But you believe me – don't you, Malcolm?" asked the vole. "It *is* raining."

The mallard cocked an eye to the sky. "Well, but, I mean," he mumbled, "thing is, see, it's always raining, isn't it? A little rain doesn't make a flood." The duck hurried after his friends. "Got to run. See you, Jeremy!"

Malcolm was right. It *was* always raining this time of year. It could rain for days on end – and often did! – and it still did not add up to the smallest ripple of a flood.

Jeremy felt small and stupid and foolish. He paddled slowly downstream to his best sunning branch and climbed out of the water to sit and drip miserably in the rain. It came to him, as he sat there all soggy, that this was where the heron had spoken to him.

"I wish I'd never heard of the Great Blue Heron," he muttered, stroking the water from his fur with his paws. "I'm a laughing-stock – an outcast! And it's all because of him."

He was still sitting there, feeling sorry for himself, when he heard a soft hissing in his ear. He turned to see a thin green grass snake slipping down the bank to the water. "Oh, hello, Glynnis," he said unhappily.

"Hello, Jeremy," replied the green snake. "Why so sssad?"

"You mean you haven't heard what a fool I am?"

"Should I have?"

Jeremy shrugged. "I thought all of Riverbank knew by now. The swans and ducks are having a good laugh."

"Don't mind them. You know what they're like," soothed the snake. "Besidesss, to a fool all things are foolish." Glynnis regarded the vole closely. "Surely, it isn't ssso bad."

"Bad enough. There was a picnic basket and I – " he broke off with a groan. "What's the use? They're right – I am a fool for believing in the heron."

"The heron – you mean the Great Blue Heron?"

"That's the one," said Jeremy. "How did you know?"

"I guesssed," replied Glynnis slyly. "Tell me more."

Jeremy took a deep breath and began to tell the grass snake about the heron and his message and all that had happened as a result. When he finished, he said, "Now I suppose you think I'm a fool, too, for believing all this nonsense about blue herons and floods."

"I don't sssee that it mattersss what I think," said Glynnis. "The point isss: can you be more of a fool than you already are?"

Jeremy thought for a moment. "No," he answered at last. "I don't see how."

"Well then," said the snake, "there you are."

"Where is that exactly?" wondered Jeremy, a little puzzled. "I don't understand."

"You must," whispered Glynnis. "Oh, you mussst." And she slithered away.

A snake's logic is often difficult to untangle, and snakes themselves don't seem to be able to explain very well. But what Glynnis seemed to be saying was that Jeremy should keep believing in the Blue Heron and do what he could to carry out his task, no matter what anybody else thought. After all, people couldn't think him more foolish than they already did. Could they?

Cold comfort there. And it didn't begin to solve his main problem: he still had to figure out how to save Riverbank.

"Oh, that!" he sniffed. "I suppose I shall have to think of something."

But what? Just then the rain, which had been pattering gently, began pelting down in a much more serious manner.

"And by the look of it," muttered Jeremy, "I shall have to think of it soon." He slipped off his branch and paddled for home.

Mr Doom-and-Gloom

"Now then," Jeremy said, munching a bit of meadow sweet, "I am no good at making speeches. That much is clear. What *can* I do?"

He sat in his snug den, listening to the rain outside. As he ate his lunch, he thought, as he had been thinking all morning: What to do? What am I going to do? Oh what, oh what, to do, to do?

"So, speeches are right out," he decided – not for the first time. "What is left?"

Leaflets! Yes! He could print up a bunch of handbills and slip one through the door of every creature on Riverbank. Danger! Warning! Flood! Big red letters. Big red CAPITAL letters! Everyone would read the notice and move to safety. Yes! Perfect! That was it!

No, that was *not* it. "No one reads leaflets," he muttered. Mostly folk just chucked them out when they came in the door. And what about all those creatures who couldn't read?

Neither speeches nor leaflets were the answer. What then? There *must* be some way of warning the others. After all, he couldn't go around banging on all the doors personally, could he? Knock, Knock! Excuse me, sir or madam, Mr Doom-and-Gloom at your service. Just stopped in to say your home is about to be swept away by a flood and you will most certainly be drowned. Good day! Well? Could he?

Of course he could! That is exactly what he *could* do. Oh, but then he would have to leave his cosy little home and go out in the rain. The rain he didn't mind so much, but he hated leaving home. The mere thought of it made his feet itch.

He looked fondly at his fine house, and his most treasured belongings. "Maybe I should wait until it stops raining," he thought. "A good night's sleep in a dry bed, a good breakfast to start the day. Yes, that's the ticket!"

No, no, best get started. The sooner he started, the sooner he would finish, and the sooner he could get back to his nice house and stay there.

Jeremy crept to the doorway and peeped out again. No change; it was still raining. The clouds hung dark and low, leaking water all over

Riverbank and the wider world beyond. The rain fell in a steady pat-pat-patter, splashing down in big, juicy drops. Just looking at the dismal scene made him feel cold and tired.

But then he glanced down at the canal running before his door. The current was swifter, and . . . WHAT? He blinked his eyes. The water had risen since the rain began. It was well up the bank now.

Gosh! thought Jeremy. If this keeps up . . . Right! Time to get busy. He ducked back into his hole, grabbed his unfinished lunch and, filling his cheeks, slipped down the bank and into the water.

A gang of swans, cruising upstream, happened past as the vole slid into the water. "Lovely weather, Jeremy!" called the leader to him. "Nothing like a little rain to freshen things up, eh?" They all snickered at this.

Jeremy turned away without a word. He could hear them laughing at him as they paddled away. "Let them laugh," he told himself, "it only shows how little they know."

He arrived in a little while at his first stop: Bodger Badger, Lord Mayor of Riverbank. If something was to be done, Mayor Badger would have to be notified. The Lord Mayor kept him waiting, of course, and appeared none too pleased when he saw it was Jeremy back again.

"Oh, it's you, Vole," grunted the badger, gazing over Jeremy's head hopefully. "I thought it might be the press. I'll just say good day to you, as I'm frightfully busy." Mayor Badger waved Jeremy away and turned back to his den.

"Just a word, Mayor Badger," piped Jeremy. "There's going to be a terrible flood. I thought you should be the first to know."

"Flood!" snapped the mayor. "Not while I am Lord Mayor, there isn't. Don't be silly. Flood? On Riverbank? That's a dirty lie! I won't stand for it."

"Then prepare to swim," remarked Jeremy. "Spread the word." He turned, scratched his nose, and scampered off.

"Wait! Wait!" barked the badger, "I can't have a flood – I'm much too busy. Come back next Thursday! I'll see if I can work you in then."

Jeremy paid no attention to the badger's whinging. He turned and hurried away. No time to lose, the Blue had told him, and he'd lost enough time already.

River Run, Water Rise

Paddling for all he was worth, Jeremy chugged upstream. It was slow going because the current was ripping along smartly now. But the vole stroked steadily and soon arrived at the grassy bank where the mallards lived.

Jeremy dreaded going to see the ducks. He figured they would give him a bad time, and he figured right. It wasn't that they were unfriendly – the mallards were pleasant enough in their queer way. But they were a rowdy flock, and horribly disorganized. They talked all the time and never paid attention to anything anybody said, quacking, quacking, quacking all over the place, always thinking they knew best and letting everybody know it, loudly and often.

The very thought of trying to deliver his warning to the ducks made his ears, nose, tail and toes tingle something awful. "Oh well," he told himself, ignoring the tingle, "best get it over with as quickly as possible."

Jeremy swam up the canal and around the bend to where the tall grass grew along the shore of Water Meadow. It was here that the ducks had their nests among the reeds and rushes. Jeremy puttered directly to the nest of his friend Malcolm. He found the big drake and his missus, each with bill tucked under wing, fast asleep.

"Ah-hem!" he coughed. The ducks did not move. "Ughghgh!" He cleared his throat, but the mallards did not so much as turn a feather. "Malcolm!" he shouted. "It's the flood, Malcolm, wake up!"

The duck stirred at last, and opened a round, green eye. "Oh, it's you, Jeremy," the drake said with a yawn. "What's up, mate?"

"I have to talk to you about the flood."

"Again?"

"Still."

The duck unfolded his wings and beat the air – buffeting the vole about the head and shoulders. "Sorry," said Malcolm, "I always do that when I wake up. Helps get the circulation going. Now, what's all this you're on about? You're going to make yourself unpopular with all this flood talk, you know."

Jeremy shrugged. "I was never very popular before."

"Anyway," continued Malcolm, "I thought you made your point at Osney Lock the other day." Malcolm grinned and nudged Jeremy with a wing tip. "C'mon, Jeremy, admit it – that was funny."

"It wasn't funny to me. I might have been killed!"

"The lads were just having a bit of fun," said Malcolm stuffily. "If you can't take a little joke, well – "

"Look, Mal," put in Jeremy quickly, "I didn't come here to talk about that. I only want to warn you about the flood – it's already started."

The drake hushed him. "Shh! Keep your voice down. We don't want to wake the whole neighbourhood."

"Yes, we do! You all have to move to higher ground. The water is ris – " He broke off because the big mallard had dived under the water and his tail feathers were waving in the air.

Malcolm surfaced with a long, green string of bladderwort in his bill. "Snack," explained the duck. "Don't mind me. You were saying?"

"I've said it," replied Jeremy. "The flood has started. The water is rising. You and your missus,

59

and all your friends and relations, had best move to higher ground at once."

"Bit difficult, that," said Malcolm, sucking down the last of his snack. "The missus has already gone to nest, you see. Most of the others as well."

"Then move the nest."

"Oh, we don't like to move it – not once she's gone to laying. It's not done."

Jeremy sighed. "Have it your way, Malcolm. But don't say I didn't warn you." The vole turned and swam off to his next stop, another nest nearby.

The other ducks were no more willing to listen than Malcolm. They were, it seems, all quite happy to stay with their nests, rain or shine, thank you very much – *if* there was to be a flood, which they heartily doubted. "And anyway," as one of them sneered, "ducks float!" Obviously, the flood would be no problem to them.

After he'd finished with the mallards, Jeremy turned upstream once more and headed for the reedy bank below Oxpens Bridge where the swans lived. If the ducks were difficult, the swans were impossible!

Swans, as everyone on Riverbank knew, were pompous and proud. They did not take kindly to anyone telling them what to do. In fact, they rather preferred it the other way around. Nevertheless, Jeremy plucked up his small courage and charged straight ahead.

He found his friend Simon sitting on the nest, watching his three cygnets, Cyril, Cecily, and Cedric, splashing about in the rain. "Hello, Mr Vole, I give you good day, sir." Simon, like most swans, was endlessly polite. Stubborn as the day is long, but proper.

"Greetings, Simon," replied Jeremy. "I won't wish you good day, because it isn't."

"Tut, tut, man! We don't want to let a little rain get us down, do we? Nonsense, sir! Rain! That's the stuff. Makes the lilies grow and all that."

"It isn't the rain I mind," began Jeremy. He saw that it was going to be a rather long haul, so cut to the heart of the matter at once. "Look, Simon, there's going to be a flood. I think it best if you and your family move to higher ground at once. I'd advise you to urge your friends and relations to do the same."

The swan curved his neck close to his chest with an air of weary understanding. "Oh, yes, I heard about this flood of yours. Osney Lock, wasn't it? Made rather a spectacle of yourself. Tut, tut. Why ever did you want to go and do that, I wonder?"

"I was only trying to help," explained Jeremy. "I have to warn everyone about the flood."

"Decent of you, Vole; decent of you. But we swans take care of ourselves. Not like some folk around here. Have you spoken to the moorhens? I really think you should. Scatterbrained the lot of them. They're just the sort who could use a bit of shaping up. Why, the way they take on – "

"Thank you for your time, Simon," interrupted Jeremy. "I've said what I came to say. Please, think about it at least."

"No need," replied the swan proudly. "This rain won't last. I expect it will be clearing up any moment now."

Jeremy turned and scooted off among the reeds. He cocked an eye to the sky. Contrary to what Simon said, the clouds seemed darker. If anything it was raining harder than ever. And the water continued to rise.

"Hurry!" Jeremy told himself. "No time to lose!"

One Small Victory

Etty Moorhen lived on a Tesco trolley, in the middle of the canal, directly below Oxpens Bridge. She had made her nest between the wheels of the overturned shopping cart. Some clever rascal had chucked the trolley in the drink and provided the moorhen family with an island home.

A soggy island home at the moment. For Jeremy found the little black moorhen standing in the middle of the trolley, nervously strutting to and fro, and clucking to herself. "Don't like this one bit," she muttered. "Not one little bit, bit, bit."

"Hello, Etty!" called Jeremy as he swam up.

"That's as may be," replied Etty tartly. "Look at my nest! Water's coming up through the floor! What am I going to do?"

"As it happens," Jeremy said, clambering up

onto the trolley, "that is what I've come to talk to you about."

"Talk? That's all you're going to do?" The hen clacked her beak in scorn. "Water leaking through the floor and all he wants to do is talk. Fine for you, but where am I to put my eggs? What will become of my brood? Answer me that!"

"Sorry, Etty. There's not much I can do for you there," the vole told her. "Besides, I don't see any brood in your nest at the moment, nor any eggs."

"Hmmph!" she sniffed, and began strutting and muttering again. "It isn't time for laying eggs just yet. I'm only getting my nest ready, aren't I. But how can I do that with water gushing up through the floor? Answer me that!"

"Actually, it's going to get worse. Much worse. It is a flood, after all. The worst in a hundred years."

The moorhen flapped her wings crossly. "Oh, thank you very much indeed!"

"No, I mean – " began Jeremy, but it was a moment before he could get a word in.

"Where are my chicks to sleep? What about my poor little hatchlings? Where am I to lay my eggs? Work my poor tailfeathers off, I do. Have you ever tried keeping body and soul together with a brood to care for? Have you ever tried – "

"Please, Etty, listen. I realize it must be difficult

for you. But the point is, it's going to be a very bad flood. You have to leave the trolley. You can't stay here. You must move to higher ground."

The moorhen jerked her head nervously from side to side. "Oh, dear! Oh, dear! Oh, dear!" she said, and might have gone on saying it, if Jeremy hadn't taken a firm hand.

"Now, then, I think we should be going." He moved to the edge of the overturned trolley.

"But what will happen to me? Where will I live? Where will I go?"

"Don't worry. You can come back here when the danger is past."

The little black moorhen strutted here and there, poking into this and that. In the end, she turned to Jeremy and said, "Oh, I don't know. Let the flood take it all. I'll make a new nest when I come back."

"Good girl, Etty," Jeremy soothed. "I'll see you to the riverbank."

"Very kind of you, Jeremy. But don't bother. I expect you're busy. You carry on."

"Well, I do have quite a few more stops to make," he allowed. And the way the water was rising, he'd have to make them quick.

"No," Etty told him, "you run on. I'll be all right."

The vole slipped into the water once more, and turned upstream. "Goodbye then," he said as he stroked away.

"Goodbye, Jeremy!" the moorhen called after him. "And thank you!"

The moorhen's thanks gave Jeremy a warm feeling as he continued on his way. "Finally," he thought to himself, "someone finally listened to me. Someone believed."

That one small victory made it easier to carry on. He paddled all the harder. The current was stronger now, the water deeper and moving faster. Jeremy soon discovered that he had to paddle almost twice as hard to move half as fast. He put his head down and set himself to some serious swimming.

Taming the Shrews

Jeremy's happy glow did not last long. His next stop took him further up the canal to a sandy patch on the bank, where brambles grew to a dense thicket. In tunnels below the brambles lived several families of shrews, sharing the thicket with a number of moles and not a few dormice.

They would be asleep this time of day, Jeremy knew, but he would have to wake them and give them the bad news. Not at all a cheery thought – bringing bad news to a cranky shrew! Oh well, it had to be done.

Jeremy paused on the bank, rain streaming down all around, wondering how best to rouse the shrews. He heard a rustling among the leaves above him and saw a very damp dormouse struggling up a dripping bramble. "Morris?" he asked, thinking he recognized the forlorn creature.

The little dormouse started, lost his grip and fell into the leaves. He got up, ready to run. "Gosh! Jeremy, you scared me witless."

"So sorry," apologized the vole. "I wasn't sure it was you. Wet dormice are much of a much to me."

"Wet!" squeaked the dormouse. "I'm soaked to the skin! My nest washed away this morning and now I've nowhere to stay until I can patch together a new one."

"That is a problem," agreed Jeremy.

"AH-CHOOOT!" sneezed Morris. "And now I'm coming down with a cold." The big-eyed dormouse shivered and sniffed. With its long, fluffy fur all soaked down, the little creature looked like a soggy mop. "You'll have to excuse me – this is not turning out a very good day."

"I'm afraid you haven't seen the worst of it," Jeremy said.

"Do tell," sighed Morris. "What else?"

So Jeremy told the dripping dormouse all about the coming flood. Morris listened, sneezing now and then, and wringing his hands. "Well, I'm not surprised. Not at all. The way things have been going, I should have expected a flood would be next. Still, it's not as if I had a nice, warm nest to worry about."

"I'm sure you'll find another nest just as nice."

"Do you think so?" said Morris, brightening somewhat.

"Definitely," replied the vole.

The dormouse shivered. "I should be going. Was there anything else?"

"Well, there is one *small* thing – I have to warn the shrews and moles, and . . ."

"And you'd rather not," guessed Morris. "I don't blame you. Tell you what: I'll wake them and tell them you have something to say. All right?"

"That would be a help."

"Don't mention it. We're all in this together."

Before Jeremy could say "Quite right!" the dormouse disappeared into a little hole in the ground beneath the brambles. Jeremy sat on his tail in a puddle, shifting from one foot to the other in the rain. Presently, he heard a quick rustling and up out of the ground came a tiny black shrew, with sharp, bright eyes and a sharper tongue.

"You've got a lot of nerve, mister," said the shrew, as she marched up to stand in front of Jeremy with her pointed little snout thrust up at him. "Just what do you think you're doing – skulking around, waking decent people at this hour? Not that we could sleep with all this rain."

The tiny shrew was joined a moment later by two others, equally upset. "Who is this big lummox?" demanded one. "Is he going to keep us standing here all day?" whined the other. "It's raining out here."

"Please," soothed Jeremy, "I'll make it as brief as I can."

"You do that, Noodle Nose," warned the first shrew. "And make it snappy!"

"That's telling him, Meg!" squeaked the second. "Teach him to come barging in here as if he owned the place!" added the third.

"Ladies, please! I've come to warn you all of the flood – "

"Flood! Flood is it? What flood is this, then?" cried Meg, jumping up and down. "We don't know anything about any stupid old flood."

"Indeed not!" sniffed the other two. "We're not having any of it!"

"Yes, I'm afraid you are," insisted Jeremy. "We all are. It's to be the worst flood in a hundred years."

"Oh, super!" screeched Meg. "Just what I need! Who's responsible for that, then? I want names and addresses, Mr Misery Guts. They are going to hear from me! I won't stand for it!"

"Us, too!" added the others. "If you think we're

going to stand for any stupid old flood, you've got another think coming!"

"But it's a flood," explained Jeremy. "No one is responsible – it just happens."

"Not around here it doesn't!" shrieked the shrew. "Who told you?"

"The Great Blue Heron told me," explained Jeremy.

"Ha! Likely story," mocked Meg. "I've never seen the Great Blue Heron, and I don't believe in anything I haven't seen."

"Believe what you like, but look for yourself – the flood has already started." Jeremy pointed to the canal; water was lapping at the very edge of the thicket. "And it's going to get much worse."

"That's what you think! Mayor Badger will hear about this."

"I'm sure he'd love to hear from you later," Jeremy suggested. "Right now you've got to move to higher ground."

Just then a bump bulged up in the sand, right at Jeremy's feet. The bump burst and out popped the fuzzy head of a mole. "Morris sent me," piped the mole. "Said you wanted to see me. A matter of some urgency, I believe."

"This jackanapes says we're having a flood!" cried Meg.

"A flood, you say? Why, that's very bad, isn't it?" said the mole. He peered around at the shrews. "G'day, ladies."

"Easy for you, Adrian!" screeched Meg. "I've got eight million things to do today. I haven't time for floods."

The two other shrews leaped at Jeremy. "If you think we have time for any floods, Jeremy Vole, you have another think coming," they shrilled.

"Please, ladies, please!" said Jeremy, trying to calm them. "You still have time to gather your things and move to higher ground."

Just then Morris reappeared to say that he'd roused the others. "They're on their way," he said, "and I'm off to my cousin Rita's – she has a raspberry patch on the towpath. I'll be safe enough there. Goodbye, all."

The mole started digging. "Right! I'll just fetch the missus and we're away, too. Jeremy, ladies, farewell."

"Hmph!" Meg tapped her foot crossly. "I suppose you think we're staying behind!"

"If you think *we're* staying behind, you have an – " began the other shrews, but Jeremy cut them off.

"Please yourself," he told them. "I have to warn

the others." Jeremy hurried away, leaving the shrews arguing on the sandy patch while water rose all around them.

12

Two Close Shaves

All along the riverbank, Jeremy told his fellow creatures about the flood, stopping only long enough to warn them and then hurrying on again. It was tiring work. Cold and wet, too; the wind was blowing harder and the rain was driving down in stinging sheets.

In no time at all Jeremy's tail, ears, and nose were all but frozen. His fur was matted and muddy, his feet ached, his stomach was empty, and he felt as if he had run ten miles in a hurricane.

He wanted to go home. He wanted nothing more than to curl up in his warm, snug den, with a nice horse-radish and cup of hot nettle tea, then nestle down in the thistle fluff, to fall asleep on his soft, dry bed. Dry . . . what a delicious word! Oh, to be dry again!

But there were still riverfolk to be warned:

frogs, ducks, a newt or two, more ducks, more swans, some snakes, a handful of hedgehogs and a multitude of mice. In fact, more creatures remained to be warned than he had warned so far. Jeremy shook the rain from his sodden pelt and proceeded on his way. At stop after stop, at nest, hole and den, he alerted the residents to the danger coming upon them.

As before, some of the creatures believed what he told them and heeded his warning. Others did not wish to be bothered. Some listened politely, others laughed at him. Sometimes he was welcomed, sometimes he was sent away with harsh words ringing in his ears. But did he become discouraged?

Yes, he did, a little. Jeremy thought that his warning – together with the wind and rain and water rising dangerously – would have been enough to convince even the most hardened doubters. But most of Riverbank's creatures did not seem the least bit interested in his warning. Either they thought it a joke, or it made them cross. So they laughed at him, or they shouted at him. This made Jeremy feel about as useful as the measles.

Yet, for the sake of the few who believed, Jeremy endured the doors slammed in his face and the jeers. He plodded on with his warning, and the rain came pouring down and the waters rose higher.

Jeremy came at last to the bridge at Oxpens Road – the furthest end of Riverbank. "Finished at last!" he sighed with relief. But even as he sat back on his hind feet to rest, his eyes stole across the canal . . . There were creatures on the other side as well. They'd drown if he didn't warn them.

"I'd better get busy," he said, then gazed at the swift-running stream before him. Empty cans and bottles bobbed along, a battered old pram, a bicycle, a biscuit tin, a broken oar, an oil drum, an inside-out umbrella, a blue welly, someone's shirt and trousers, a fish crate, and a wide assortment of branches – all of them swirling and whirling in the rising torrent.

"Gosh! I can't swim in that," Jeremy murmured. "I'd be dashed to bits in seconds. I'll have to walk." He turned to the bridge above him.

Now the bridge at Oxpens Road is very busy. There are cars and bicycles, buses and vans, taxis, trucks and lorries thundering wildly over its narrow length. Crossing such a bridge can be tricky; as a rule, Riverbank creatures do not attempt it. But Jeremy had no choice. He had to warn the creatures on the other side of the canal, and to do that he had to use the bridge.

He crept slowly up the bank and peered fearfully along the gutter awash with rain. Cars splashed by him as he crouched at the curb. "Well, it's now or never," he said to himself. "Go!"

Jeremy had scarcely set paw on the bridge when a big truck came roaring right at him. The vole scampered back, just as the big wheels whizzed by.

The wind-blast sent the vole rolling down the path. "Yow! That was a close shave," Jeremy muttered, feeling his whiskers. He picked himself up and climbed the path again. More cautious this time, he waited for a let-up in the traffic. "Right! First chance I get – "

He waited. And he waited some more. The rain drove down and the traffic rumbled like thunder, and there never did come a chance for Jeremy to cross the bridge. Once he thought he might just slip over when he saw a lone bicycle start across. But the moment he jumped out onto the bridge the bicycle rider saw him and screamed, "Rat! Rat!" and tried to run over him. Jeremy escaped only by his thinnest whisker.

"Another close shave!" complained Jeremy. "I'll never get across this way." So he turned tail and

hurried back down the footpath to the water's edge once more. He stood a long time, staring at the fast, frothy stream. "I don't want to go in there," he said at last. Just looking at all that icy water made his teeth chatter and his bones ache.

But what else could he do? The creatures on the other side of Riverbank had to be warned. And since Jeremy had begun the job, he knew he had to see it through to the end. So he hauled himself into the cold, black water, chattering teeth and all.

He took a deep breath and pushed out from the bank. Instantly, the current seized him and pulled him away. The canal ran swift and deep, and stronger than he had ever known it. Jeremy helplessly watched the far shore sliding past as the swollen canal hurled him recklessly along.

Jeremy swam as never before, pumping his legs and dodging the trash and debris. Branches crashed into him, cans and bottles bashed him about, but Jeremy gritted his teeth and kept paddling. Dashed first this way and then another, he steered as best he could for the far shore. Whirlpools sucked at him and turned him around; big waves splashed over him; the current dragged him down. Though the opposite bank did not seem to be getting any closer, he did not turn back. Instead, he closed his eyes and chugged away – one little vole, swimming for his life.

13

One Foot in Front of the Other

Legs churning, heart thumping, Jeremy swam. All his muscles ached, and his skin and fur and bones. But he did not dare stop now or he would surely drown. The canal had turned into a torrent. Rain beat down on him, stinging his eyes. OOPH! An empty milk bottle smacked him in the ribs. YOW! A sharp stick poked his spine. OUCH! A piece of driftwood slammed into his shoulder. Still he kept swimming. His legs pumped and his feet paddled and his tail waved back and forth. Only the tip of his nose showed above water. Soon not even that.

Just when he thought he could not swim another stroke, Jeremy felt solid ground under his toes. He opened his eyes and saw that he had reached the far shore at last.

Bruised, battered, bumped this way and that by the floating debris, he had reached the other side.

He was so tired he could hardly stagger from the water.

A voice came to him. It was the voice of the Great Blue Heron and it seemed to be speaking to him. *One foot in front of the other,* the voice said, *that's all it takes — one foot in front of the other. Chin up, you're doing fine.*

So, putting one foot in front of the other, Jeremy dragged himself from the canal — and then promptly collapsed on the muddy bank, where he lay for a moment in a heap. "Whew!" he gasped, "I made it!"

Jeremy could not rest long. Now that he had reached the other side he had work to do. "As soon as I've finished," he promised himself, "I will curl up in my soft bed and not set foot outside for a week."

He raised himself slowly and hobbled off along the muddy track beneath the footpath. He came first to a huddle of harvest mice, all crowded together in one corner of their ruined nest; most of it had washed away and they were too frightened to go out and search for any other shelter. Jeremy explained about the flood, but the mice wouldn't listen. "It will stop raining soon," they said. "The sun will come out and dry up all the water and we will be safe."

"No, you won't be safe," Jeremy told them. "The flood will get worse. This place will be under water soon. You have to move to higher ground."

"We can't!" screeched the mice. "We have nowhere else to go."

"Anywhere else is better than here," Jeremy declared. "Climb a fence; climb a tree. Go and find a hole in a wall near the footpath. You will be safe there."

The mice heard him, yet insisted that they would stay in their ruined nest, with water sloshing and surging all around them. Jeremy couldn't understand why they preferred drowning to moving, and he tried to convince them to leave. But it was no use. He hurried on to warn others.

The frogs he visited next wouldn't hear a word he said. They just laughed at him and hopped away, saying, "Who's afraid? Who's afraid? Who's afraid of a silly old flood?"

The ducks nearby were of much the same opinion as the mice and frogs: that everything was going to be all right and that there was really nothing to worry about. "Go home, Vole," they told him. "No sense in getting all worked up over a bit of rain. You are making a fool of yourself. Go home and leave us alone."

But, much as he would have liked to, the determined little vole did not go home. He plodded on until he had warned everyone on the far side of the canal, eventually covering the entire distance from Oxpens Bridge to the Water Meadow footbridge, past that and on to the Gas Bridge and beyond. Every step of the way on very sore feet – he wasn't used to so much walking!

He warned those he knew well, and some he'd never met before. He warned young and old, fast and slow, feathered, finned and furred. He warned them all.

At last he reached the end of the footpath at Friars Wharf and stood peering into the stinging rain. He had finished; there were no more creatures to be warned. He turned around slowly, and, placing one sore, heavy foot in front of the other, he started for home at last.

But he hadn't dragged himself more than a few steps when he stopped short. "Admiral Reggie!" cried Jeremy. "I almost forgot." Jeremy turned right around and bustled off into the rain once more.

14

Informing the Admiral

Muddy, and panting for breath, Jeremy limped down the track to a little hump of earth in the bank beside a big old alder tree. On the side of the hump nearest the water was the entrance to the burrow of Rear-Admiral Reginald King-Fisher (retired), who lived there with his wife and a crew of little kingfishers.

Jeremy rapped politely at the door. He waited. No answer. He knocked again. No one seemed to be at home. "I suppose," murmured Jeremy, "they've already moved off."

Jeremy turned to leave, but a crusty voice called him back. "Halt! Who goes there?"

"It's Jeremy Vole, sir."

"What is the meaning of this unseemly racket? Explain yourself, man."

"Glad I caught you, Admiral King-Fisher. I'm warning everyone about the flood, and I – "

"Attention!" crackled the kingfisher. "Shoulders back! Stand up straight! Don't mumble! If you have something to say, Sunshine, say it!"

"Yes, sir!" Jeremy snapped to attention.

"That's better. Now then, what's this all about? I believe I heard the word 'flood' in your mutterings."

"Yes, sir! A terrible flood, sir. I've come to warn you to take evasive action, sir!"

"Flood? I don't recall approving any flood."

"No, sir! It is a voluntary flood, sir!"

"Impossible! On whose authority?"

"I have it on highest authority, sir."

"From the top brass, is it?" The kingfisher cocked his head to one side. "That's all right, then. When is this flood operation to take place, Vole?"

"At once, sir."

The admiral poked his sharp beak into the air and looked at the foul sky; then he cast his bright eye on the rising stream. "Great Scott! The water is almost up to my door! Why wasn't I informed?"

"I have just informed you, sir," Jeremy confirmed.

"Quite! Well, you are doing a fine job. I will make a note of it in my report. Carry on, Vole!"

"Aye, Aye, Admiral!" Jeremy saluted, but the

kingfisher had already dived back inside and he could hear the admiral squawking orders to his wife and children.

"Well, that's that – finished at last," said Jeremy, turning away. "Now, I can go home . . ."

He watched the racing water. It had not yet reached the top of the riverbank. "If I hurry," he said to himself, "I will have just enough time to move my things to higher ground and all will be safe."

Cold, footsore, weary through and through, Jeremy started back along the path to the Water Meadow footbridge. It took him a long time to walk all that way in the driving rain, but he didn't dare try to swim again. The dismal day grew even more gloomy as he lumbered on. By the time he reached the footbridge, darkness had begun to fall. Shivering, he started across.

Inch by inch, he climbed. The rain beat down; the wild wind screamed. Jeremy, ears flat to his head and teeth clenched against the cold, hauled himself up the steep slope of the high-arching bridge. Upon gaining the crest, he took a step forward, looked down the other side . . . and stopped dead in his tracks.

The far end of the bridge was sunk deep in water.

Jeremy could not believe his eyes. All of Water Meadow was a great, ghastly, grey torrent of surging, swelling water. The reeds and rushes and grasses were gone. Gone, too, the footpath and riverbank. The meadow was one enormous mass of angry chop and froth, from the footpath behind him to the towpath on the far side of River. The vole stood blinking at the wind-whipped waves and his heart sank.

He had come too late. His fine house was gone. Wrecked, wiped out, washed away. No more snug den, no more soft downy bed, no more bulging pantry. No more nice house. The one place Jeremy loved best in all the world was a mud-filled ruin. He had lost everything.

Too busy saving others, he had forgotten to save himself.

Jeremy plopped down right in the middle of the bridge and cried. He had reached the end of his endurance. He was cold to the bone and his bones were cold, too. The rain pelted down on him, soaking him through and through. He sat on the bridge in the rain, one miserable, homeless little vole.

Well, he had to do something. He couldn't just sit on the bridge and wait for the flood to carry that away, too. So, after a little while, he got to his aching feet and lugged his water-logged carcass back down the bridge to the footpath.

Across the footpath stood a long brick wall. Jeremy trudged along the wall until he found a nook where a broken brick had come loose. Heartsick and numb, he crawled in, wrapped his tail around his feet and closed his tired eyes.

Disaster!

Huddled in his little nook, Jeremy did not sleep a wink the whole long, dreadful night. Instead, he listened to the howling wind and the lashing rain and the roaring, angry flood water.

When daylight came, Jeremy poked his head from his cramped little crevice and peered fearfully out. The sky was still a mass of low, dark clouds and the rain still pelted down. "I'd better go and see what is happening," he said, and crept cautiously out from his crack in the wall.

He did not have to creep very far, however; the damage became apparent to him at once. It was a disaster!

Everywhere he looked, branches and limbs were down, and along the footpath three big trees had toppled over one another. Part of a garden wall had collapsed, spilling bricks across the footpath. Down by the footbridge, a log had become trapped, causing a mountain of trash and debris to build up behind it. Turning to Riverbank, Jeremy gasped at what he saw: a huge, grey, ugly, dangerous sea, filled with scum and muck and junk, tumbling along recklessly. Riverbank had been swept away completely.

The nests of the ducks and swans among the reeds would have been the first to go – followed by the dens further up the bank, and then the burrows in the meadow. Nests, lairs, warrens and holes everywhere were swallowed up, covered over, and destroyed. The homeless of Riverbank had taken what refuge they could find in the long grass beside the footpath. There, huddled in the cold and dark, they had waited until morning.

"The worst disaster in a hundred years," whispered Jeremy, gazing grimly around at the destruction. "The Great Blue Heron was right."

The fact that the Great Blue Heron was proved right in the end – and that Jeremy was wise to believe him – did not cheer the vole one little bit. The disaster was too terrible, the damage too great for any 'I told you so' sort of cheer. Riverbank, his home and everybody else's, was a horrible ruin. There was no room in his heart for anything but sadness.

16

A Bitter Crust

Jeremy decided to go along the footpath to see how his friends had weathered the storm. Hobbling slowly on his sore feet, he started off and soon came to a clump of ducks, squatting in a nettle patch at the edge of the footpath.

The ducks lifted their heads as he approached, but none of them quacked so much as a sorrowful greeting. As Jeremy came closer, one of the ducks said, "I suppose you're happy now."

"Happy? No, I – " began Jeremy.

"Well, you can just go and gloat somewhere else. You think you're so high and mighty," muttered another of the ducks. "Shove off!" said a third.

"We've lost our nests and our egglings," sniffed a mother duck. "We're devastated!"

"I know how you feel," said Jeremy, and he meant it. "I lost my house, too."

"Get going," said the first duck. "We don't need you around here – taking on so superior-like. Go away!"

Jeremy did move on. He came next to a knot of mice clinging to some brambles. "Look!" whispered one of them to the others. "There's that crazy vole. Here he comes!"

Instantly, the mice pretended to be asleep. Jeremy tried waking them, but they insisted on pretending, so he continued on a little further and found the shrews with their soggy children hidden among the wet leaves beneath a hawthorn thicket. "Sorry to intrude," the vole said, "but I just came by to see that you are all right."

"Of course we're not all right!" wailed Meg. "We're half drowned, thanks to you!"

"If you think we're all right," shrieked the others, "you've got another think coming!"

"You and your flood!" Meg shouted. "We were perfectly happy before you came along. Now everything is ruined! Where are my children to sleep? What are we going to eat? It's all your fault, Jeremy Vole!"

"I'm sorry," Jeremy told her. "Very, very sorry . . ."

Simon and Sylvia Swan and the cygnets were camped in the long grass nearby. Simon raised

his head and hissed, "Bad enough that we've lost our home. We don't need you coming round here saying 'I told you so!' Get on with you."

"But I'm *not* saying 'I told you so' – really, I'm not," explained Jeremy. "I lost my home, too, you know. I'm as sorry as anyone about what happened."

"It's different for you," Sylvia insisted. *"You're* the one who saw the Great Blue Heron, so that's all right then. I'm not at all certain I care for your attitude." She turned her head away.

"Sorry . . ." muttered Jeremy, as he walked away.

All along the footpath, Jeremy found the creatures of Riverbank tucked away in this little nook, or that little cranny. A few, like Etty Moorhen and Admiral King-Fisher (retired), greeted him and thanked him for warning them. But most of the others seemed to think that the flood was Jeremy's fault and they blamed *him* for the disaster.

His friend Malcolm was no different. "None of this would have happened if you hadn't poked your nose into it," the big duck complained. "We've lost everything because of you."

"Because of me!" cried Jeremy. "I tried to *warn* you!"

"Well, you should have tried harder," declared Malcolm. "Now look what's happened: our nest is washed away and our egglings are lost. The missus is horrible upset – grieving she is. Taking on something awful. Nor do I blame her. It's a bitter crust, that's what it is – a bitter crust."

"I'm sorry," said Jeremy. That's all he *could* say – and he seemed to be saying it to everyone.

By late afternoon he arrived back at his temporary quarters, the nook in the wall. His head ached from all the complaining he had heard, and his heart was sore from the abuse. He was discouraged and unhappy, and feeling as if he'd made the biggest mistake of his life in listening to the heron.

"Nothing good has come of it," he muttered, as he dragged himself into his nook. "Malcolm is right: it *is* a bitter crust." Taking the tip of his tail in his front feet, he sat staring forlornly out on the disaster.

Jeremy did not stir for the rest of the day. Nor did he come out the next day. He was simply too discouraged and unhappy.

17

Local Hero

The sun peeked out for a short while on the third day. But when it saw what a mess the flood had made, it quickly hid itself behind the clouds again. Riverbank *was* a mess – and getting messier as the flood waters slowly retreated.

There was a sheen of thick, black mud over everything; shrubs had been uprooted and trees toppled; great hunks of the riverbank had been carved out and carried off; reeds, rushes and thickets were flattened; branches, limbs and logs were piled higgledy-piggledy where the angry flood waters had tossed them.

Jeremy crawled out from his nook in the wall to sit at the edge of the footpath and stare unhappily at the destruction. He looked for his house on the bank, but it, like everything else, was washed clean away; he could not even see where the front door had been. He would have to start from scratch and build a new home.

By evening of the third day the flood waters had receded enough for Jeremy to swim across to the riverbank. He puttered about on the bank for some time, searching here and there in the muck. But he could not find a single trace of his fine house. He was just about to go back to his refuge in the wall when he heard a rustle of feathers and turned around to see two long poles sticking out of the water where no poles ought to be . . .

"Oh, no!" gasped Jeremy. "It can't be – " As he spoke, his beady little eyes travelled up the long length of the poles to see the body of a bird perched at the very top – a huge, keen-eyed, long-necked, sharp-beaked, stilt-legged, blue-feathered bird. Yes, it was the Great Blue Heron. And it was watching him closely.

"Why so glum, chum?" asked the Great Blue.

"As if you didn't know," sniffed Jeremy. "I'm in a lot of trouble because of you. Everyone blames me for this – this mess." He lifted his paw to the flooded ruin around him.

"Because of me?" wondered the Heron. "Do you mean to tell me, Vole," he said, clicking his beak sharply, "that you think *I* am the cause your friends' complaints?"

"Who else?" Jeremy's fur bristled. "It's true!

They all hate me now, and it's all because I listened to you. I wish I'd never told any of them about the flood."

"They are upset," the Great Blue Heron soothed. "Give them a day or two and they'll begin to see things differently."

"But they think it's *my* fault. They've all lost their homes and nests and eggs and things, and they blame me," grumbled Jeremy.

"I told you it wouldn't be easy," remarked the heron. "But never mind, you did the right thing."

"Humph!" the unhappy vole grunted. "Who cares?"

"If it makes you feel any better," the Great Blue continued, "your friends are alive today because of you. Think of that. Out of all the creatures on Riverbank, I chose you. And I'm glad I did."

"Chose me? *I* bumped into *you* by accident."

"Oh, I don't believe in accidents, Jeremy," the Great Blue Heron replied. "I gave you a difficult and important job because I knew you were the one to do it. Who else?"

Jeremy shrugged. "Anyone else."

"Come now," the Blue Heron chided. "Would Malcolm have listened? Or Alfred? Can you see Mayor Badger waddling up and down Riverbank warning everyone? Or one of the swans? Now, tell me the truth: can you imagine *any* of the others sticking to it like you did?"

"No," Jeremy admitted finally, "I suppose not."

"You were the only one, Jeremy."

It was true – no one else would have done what Jeremy Vole did. The Lord Mayor was much too busy, and Riggs Rabbit couldn't be bothered. Others, like Alfred Hedgehog and the frogs, didn't even believe in the Great Blue Heron. And the swans were far too superior to go racing all over the place. Easygoing Malcolm would have thought it too much trouble; besides, no duck would have stuck his neck out for another. Admiral King-Fisher would have demanded orders in triplicate through the Proper Channels before twitching a feather. Etty Moorhen might have been willing, but she wasn't up to the task, poor thing. And the shrews, mice, moles? Never in a million years.

"You'll just have to face it," the Great Blue Heron declared. "Jeremy Vole, you are a hero."

"Now you're making fun of me," replied the vole. "You know I'm no hero."

"Oh?" The Great Blue looked surprised. "Then what would you call someone who risked life and limb for the safety of others? Tell me, Jeremy –

what would you call someone who braved great danger and endured enormous hardship to save his fellow creatures?" The Great Blue Heron regarded the vole proudly. "I don't know about you, but *I* call that someone a hero."

"A hero . . ." wondered the little vole. "You really think so?"

"I do," said the Great Blue. "And as soon as the others have finished feeling sorry for themselves, they will think so, too. You'd better get used to it."

This surprised Jeremy more than anything the Heron had said so far. "I do believe you mean it."

"They'll be singing your praises from one end of Riverbank to the other." The big blue bird unfolded his wings and stretched them wide. "I'm never wrong about these things, you know."

"Gosh!"

"But none of that matters," the Great Blue continued. "Whether they thank you or blame you is all the same in the end. The important thing is that you listened, you believed, and you did something about it."

The Great Blue Heron reached out with a wing tip and stroked the little vole on the head. "Well done, Jeremy, my boy. I'm proud of you."

Jeremy didn't know what to say. But he felt his sadness melting away and a huge happy smile slowly spreading across his face.

The heron began flapping his wings. "It's time for me to go. Remember what I said."

"Wait!" cried the vole. "Don't leave yet. I want some of the others to meet you!"

"Farewell, Jeremy!" the Great Blue told him. Then, lifting his long, stilt legs, he took a few running steps across the water and launched himself into the air.

The vole swam after him. "Will I ever see you again?" he cried.

The Great Blue Heron flew up and circled over the canal. "I might pop in again some time," the heron called back. "You never can tell."

"Goodbye!" Jeremy said, and watched as the great blue bird disappeared – a bright flash of blue through the trees and he was gone.

New Digs

Bright and early the next morning, Jeremy set about building a new home. He chose a good place, well up on the bank, and began digging. He dug the entrance and the tunnel, and was just beginning the den when who should come quacking up but Malcolm. "Halloo, Jeremy!"

"Oh, hello, Malcolm. I didn't think you'd ever speak to me again."

"Uh, listen, mate, I'm sorry about that. Thing is, I was a bit upset," confessed the big drake. "I know it wasn't really your fault. Why, you lost your house same as the rest of us." Malcolm looked at the hole in the riverbank. "New digs?"

"Yes," answered the vole. "Like everyone else, I'm starting all over again."

"That's just what I was saying," Malcolm replied. "I told the missus, 'I'll bet ol' Jeremy's building a new house today, just like us.' So, she said, 'Why don't you take him a little fluff for his bed?' And here I am." With that, the mallard bent down and plucked a big bunch of feathers from his chest. "How's that?"

"Why, that's very thoughtful of you, Malcolm," the vole said, surprised by such a generous gift. "But you didn't have to do that for me."

"Think nothing of it, my friend. It's the least I can do – after you tried to warn us and all. Is that enough? If you need more, just whistle."

Jeremy took the feathery down in his paws. "Thanks, Mal. This will make a very snug bed."

"What are friends for?" quacked Malcolm. "Well, I'm off. Me and the missus have a new nest to finish and another clutch to lay. See you!"

"I'll see you, Malcolm," called Jeremy. He put the duck feathers to one side and continued with his work. He finished the den and started in on the pantry, slaving away until he remembered he hadn't had a single bite to eat in days. "There's nothing at all to eat here," he said, regarding his empty pantry. "I'll have to go out and see if I can scavenge anything."

Just as Jeremy poked his head outdoors, he saw Simon and Sylvia Swan swimming. "Hi-ho, Vole," called Simon. "Good to see you. Busy as usual, I see."

"Good to see you, too," replied the vole, cautiously. Last time he'd seen the swans they had sent him away with harsh words. "And, yes, I'm just finishing a bit of digging."

"Malcolm stopped by and said you were building a new home," said Simon. "That's hungry work, I know – we've been feathering our new nest all morning."

"So we've brought you a little something," said Sylvia sweetly. She dropped a leaf-wrapped bundle at his feet. "Call it a peace offering. We're sorry about the way we treated you. It wasn't fair. After all, you did your best to help us; we just didn't listen."

Jeremy unwrapped the bundle and out rolled a clove of wild garlic.

"You can't make a meal of garlic," piped a shrill little voice. Jeremy turned to see the shrews scampering down the riverbank. Each one held a sprig of spearmint which she placed beside the garlic. "There," said Meg with a smile, "now *that's* a nice lunch."

"Thank you," murmured Jeremy, becoming embarrassed by all the fuss. "It's very kind of you all."

"Got to run, Vole," said Simon, paddling slowly off. "Do come round for lunch once you're settled

in, won't you? We're friends, you know, and we don't see nearly enough of one another."

This is how it went the rest of the day. Every time Jeremy turned around there was someone at his door with a little something – a sprig of this, a bite of that, small bits and bobs for his house, a kind word, or an apology. Alfred and Riggs came to see him, and the dormice and kingfishers, the mallards and moorhens and moles. Even the Lord Mayor dropped by with an official 'Job Well Done' for helping save voters from the disaster.

Well, with everyone stopping by all day, Jeremy had a terrible time getting his new house built. But, all in all, he really didn't mind. And it wasn't until he crawled into his downy bed to sleep that he realized he hadn't itched for days. Somehow, he didn't mind that, either.

A NOTE TO YOUNG NATURALISTS

While most of the creatures in this book can be found along any typical riverbank in Britain, a few (such as Great Blue Herons and turtles), are not natives. I put them in because nature, as you know, is full of surprises.

THE AUTHOR